# SHERLOCK HOLMES

## AND THE

## HORROR OF FRANKENSTEIN

### A GRAPHIC NOVELISATION

**WRITER**
**Luke Benjamen Kuhns**

**ARTIST**
**Marcie Klinger**

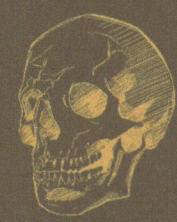

IF YOU LOOK CLOSE ENOUGH, AND THROUGH THE MESS YOUR BOYS ALREADY MADE, YOU CAN SEE THIS MAN'S FOOTPRINTS. HIS STRIDE WAS AVERAGE. HE STOPPED HERE WHERE SOMETHING TOOK HIM BY THE NECK, STRANGLED HIM, AND TOSSED HIM. NOW, IF SOMETHING HAD JUST TOSSED HIM, THAT WOUND ON HIS HEAD, THOUGH PAINFUL WOULD NOT RENDER HIM UNCONSCIOUS. SO IT IS HIGHLY UNLIKELY HE WAS PUSHED THEN STRANGLED

MAYBE IT WAS A GANG?

COME NOW. GIVEN THE THAT THERE ARE NO OTHER PRINTS HERE BESIDE THE ONES MADE BY YOUR MEN AND THE DEADMAN WE CAN RULE OUT A GANG.

IN FACT I PUT OUR KILLER AT ABOUT EIGHT FEET TALL WITH ENORMOUS HANDS AND FEET.

HOW ON EARTH CAN YOU SAY THAT, HOLMES!

WE HAVE THEIR FOOTPRINT.

BY JOVE! HOW DID YOU SEE THAT?

I SAW IT BECAUSE I WAS LOOKING FOR IT.

AND I ALSO JUDGE THAT WHOEVER THEY WERE TOOK THE BODY FROM THIS CRYPT, IS THAT CORRECT?

INDEED, IT IS. A YOUNG GIRL. JUST PUT IN YESTERDAY.

YESTERDAY, YOU SAY? THAT IS CURIOUS.

SO WHERE DO WE START? WE'RE LOOKING FOR SOME GIANT MAN ROAMING GRAVEYARDS AT NIGHT. SURELY HE CAN'T BE TOO HARD TO FIND.

INDEED, WE ARE! LET US RETURN TO BAKER STREET, I NEED TO GATHER MORE DATA!

MAGNIFICENT!!

WHAT IN BLAZES, HOLMES! IS EVERYTHING ALL RIGHT?

INDEED IT IS, OLD BOY. I HAVE MADE A DISCOVERY!

THERE IS SOMETHING UNIQUE ABOUT EACH GRAVE ROBBERY. WATSON, YOU WERE FOLLOWING THE STORY IN THE PAPERS, CAN YOU TELL ME WHAT ITS UNIQUE QUALITY IS?

OTHER THAN BEING MORBIDLY GROTESQUE, I CANNOT SAY.

WOMEN!

EACH GRAVE ROBBED BELONGED TO A WOMAN. HERE LOOK AT THIS!

SEE HERE, WATSON, THE GRAVES IN WHITECHAPEL, SAINT PANCRAS OLD CHURCH, TOWER HAMLETS, AND NOW NUNHEAD, EACH BELONGED TO A WOMAN BUT NOT JUST ANY WOMAN, ONE OF NOBLE AND WEALTHY BACKGROUND.

FOR WHAT REASON WOULD THESE GRAVES BE ROBBED? FOR BURIED RICHES?

THAT CROSSED MY MIND BUT THEN I FOUND SOMETHING VERY INTERESTING!

ACCORDING TO THE OFFICIAL REPORTS THE ONLY THINGS STOLEN WERE THE BODIES AND EVERYTHING ELSE WAS LEFT BEHIND, EVEN THE CLOTHES WERE LEFT BEHIND.

OH YES, OF COURSE. I FOUND THAT MOST DISTURBING NOW THAT I RECALL WHY TAKE THE BODIES AND LEAVE THE RICHES BEHIND? JUST DISGUSTING.

THERE IS A PATTERN TO THESE ROBBERIES, WATSON. SEEMS I WAS MISTAKEN TO IGNORE THE STORIES.

I DID TELL YOU, HOLMES!

NEVER MIND THAT NOW. THE PATTERN THAT I'VE DISCOVERED IS THUS:

**TOWER HAMLETS CEMETERY ROBBED!**

*Third Grave Robbery in 6 weeks! Who is behind it?*

**GRAVE IN WHITECHAPEL ROBBED!**

**BODY TAKEN**

THE DAILY LONDON

ST PANCRAS OLD CHURCH GRAVE ROBBED - BODY MISSING

WITH EACH ROBBERY THE BODIES BECOME MORE FRESH. THE FIRST FEW WERE WOMEN DEAD AT LEAST A DECADE. BUT THE LAST TWO WERE BOTH WOMEN THAT WERE IN THEIR GRAVES A DAY, TWO AT MOST. BUT BEYOND THAT EACH GRAVE BELONGED TO A WOMAN OF NOBILITY AND WEALTH.

WHAT DOES IT MEAN?

THAT IS WHAT WE MUST FIND OUT!

THAN WHAT IS OUR NEXT MOVE?

BY A STROKE OF LUCK, A YOUNG WOMAN, NAMED ISABELLE HAWTHORN, IS TO BE BURIED IN WEST HAM CEMETERY TOMORROW. SHE IS OF NOBLE LINEAGE AND COMES FROM A WEALTHY FAMILY.

HARDLY A STROKE OF LUCK, HOLMES!

I DO RECALL THE NAME.

SHE'S THE DAUGHTER OF LORD HAWTHORN. TRAGIC REALLY, THE POOR GIRL DIED OF CONSUMPTION IT SEEMS. BUT WHAT IS THE PLAN?

NEVERTHELESS, WATSON, SHE MAKES THE IDEAL TARGET IF THESE ROBBERS ARE LOOKING FOR BODIES WITH THE LEAST AMOUNT OF DECAY. SO YOU AND I MUST STAKE OUT IN THE GRAVEYARD TOMORROW NIGHT! IT'S BOUND TO BE COLD AND WET, SO DRESS WARMLY!

GET READY, WE'RE LEAVING IN FIVE MINUTES!

WHERE ARE WE GOING??!!

CHOP, CHOP!

WHY DID YOU DRAG ME OUT OF BED, HOLMES?

WE NEED TO SPEAK WITH A MISS VICTORIA WALTON.

VICTORIA WALTON? WHO IS SHE?

SOMEONE WHO MIGHT BE ABLE TO SHED LIGHT ON THE HORRIFIC EVENTS OF LAST NIGHT.

MAY I HELP YOU?

I BELIEVE YOU CAN. I AM SHERLOCK HOLMES AND THIS IS DOCTOR JOHN WATSON. WE NEED TO SPEAK WITH YOU REGARDING A MOST SENSITIVE TOPIC WHICH IS CONNECTED TO YOU GRANDFATHER, CAPTAIN ROBERT WALTON.

OH DEAR! WHAT IS IT ABOUT?

FRANKENSTEIN'S MONSTER...

MISS WALTON, WHAT CAN YOU TELL ME OF THE FRANKENSTEIN MONSTER?

NO ONE HAS MENTIONED THAT NAME IN DECADES.

WHAT OR WHO IS FRANKENSTEIN?

IT IS ALL LEGEND NOWADAYS, WATSON.

HOWEVER, I REMEMBER READING ONCE THAT MISS WALTON'S GRANDFATHER POSSESSED PAPERS WHICH DOCUMENTED A SO-CALLED MONSTER ATTACK IN GENEVA BACK IN 1818, BUT HE NEVER DISCLOSED THEM.

WHAT MAKES YOU THINK I KNOW WHERE THEY ARE?

ELEMENTARY. YOU ARE THE ONLY DIRECT DESCENDENT.

IF THE EVENTS WERE TRUE AND SO TERRIBLY TERRIFYING HE'D KEEP THE PAPERS LOCKED AWAY AND PASS THEM ON TO HIS NEXT OF KIN. WHICH IS YOU.

AND WHY DO YOU WANT TO KNOW?

BECAUSE I BELIEVE THE MONSTER IS IN LONDON!

WHO DO YOU THINK THIS MAN WAS THAT WANTED INFORMATION FROM MISS WALTON?
I'M NOT SURE, WATSON, BUT SOMETHING I'M SURE OF IS THAT IT IS NO COINCIDENCE THAT MISS WALTON IS QUESTIONED ABOUT THIS MONSTER IN THE MIDST OF THESE SUSPICIOUS GRAVE ROBBERIES. AND IT SEEMS FRIGHTFULLY CLEAR WHAT IS GOING ON.
WHICH IS?
SOMEONE IS CONSTRUCTING THE MONSTER'S BRIDE.
SO YOU DON'T THINK WE ARE REALLY AFTER A MONSTER?
ANY PERSON WHO BELIEVES THAT THEY CAN CREATE LIFE OUT OF THE DEAD IS ALREADY MONSTROUS, MARK MY WORDS.
WHAT I STILL DON'T KNOW IS WHAT INCLINED YOU TO GO AND SEE THIS MISS WALTON?
WHEN WE RETURNED LAST NIGHT I COULDN'T GET THAT CREATURE OUT OF MY MIND AND I RECALLED AN OLD GERMAN MYTH ABOUT A MAN-LIKE MONSTER WHO TORTURED A SMALL VILLAGE IN GENEVA, BUT OF COURSE THE WITNESSES WERE THIN AND IT PASSED INTO FOLKLORE.
BUT I WAS FORTUNATE ENOUGH TO HAVE A CATALOG OF NAMES THAT WERE ASSOCIATED WITH THIS SUPPOSED REAL EVENT, AND THE TWO MAIN NAMES BEING FRANKENSTEIN AND WALTON. WITHIN MY CATALOG I HAD STORED A NEWSPAPER CLIPPING FROM THE DAY CAPTAIN WALTON DIED WHICH TALKED ABOUT HIS CONNECTION TO THIS FOLKTALE, AND THOUGH HE HAS APPARENT PAPER DOCUMENTATION REGARDING THE EVENTS, HE REFUSED TO SHARE THEM PUBLICLY.
OUTSTANDING, HOLMES!! YOUR HABITUAL HABITS FOR STORING USELESS PILES OF PAPERS AND NOTES HAS MOST CERTAINLY PAID OFF.
IT IS NOT USELESS TO RETAIN A PLETHORA OF INFORMATION WHICH CAN BE MADE READILY AVAILABLE UPON REQUEST.
NOW COME, WATSON, IT'S TIME WE SET A TRAP!
THE DAILY TELEGRAPH

DO YOU THINK THIS WILL WORK?

THIS IS LIKE CHEESE TO A MOUSE, WATSON. THEY WON'T BE ABLE TO RESIST. THEY ARE SEARCHING FOR THE BEST IN FEMALE SPECIMEN SO WE ARE GIVING THEM ONE. BESIDES WE FOILED THEIR LAST ATTEMPT WHEN YOU TRIED TO IGNITE THE CREATE WITH THE LANTERN.

QUITE RIGHT, HOLMES.

HOW DO YOU KNOW THEY'LL READ THE ARTICLE THAT WE POSTED IN THE DAILY TELEGRAPH?

BECAUSE THEY SCOUR FOR INFORMATION ABOUT RECENT DEATHS, HOW ELSE WOULD THEY KNOW ABOUT THE GRAVES WHICH THEY WERE ROBBING? THEY ARE PLANNERS, WATSON, THEY DON'T SIMPLY STUMBLE UPON SOMETHING THEY WANT.

COME, WATSON, LET US HIDE!

IT WILL BE ANOTHER LONG NIGHT.

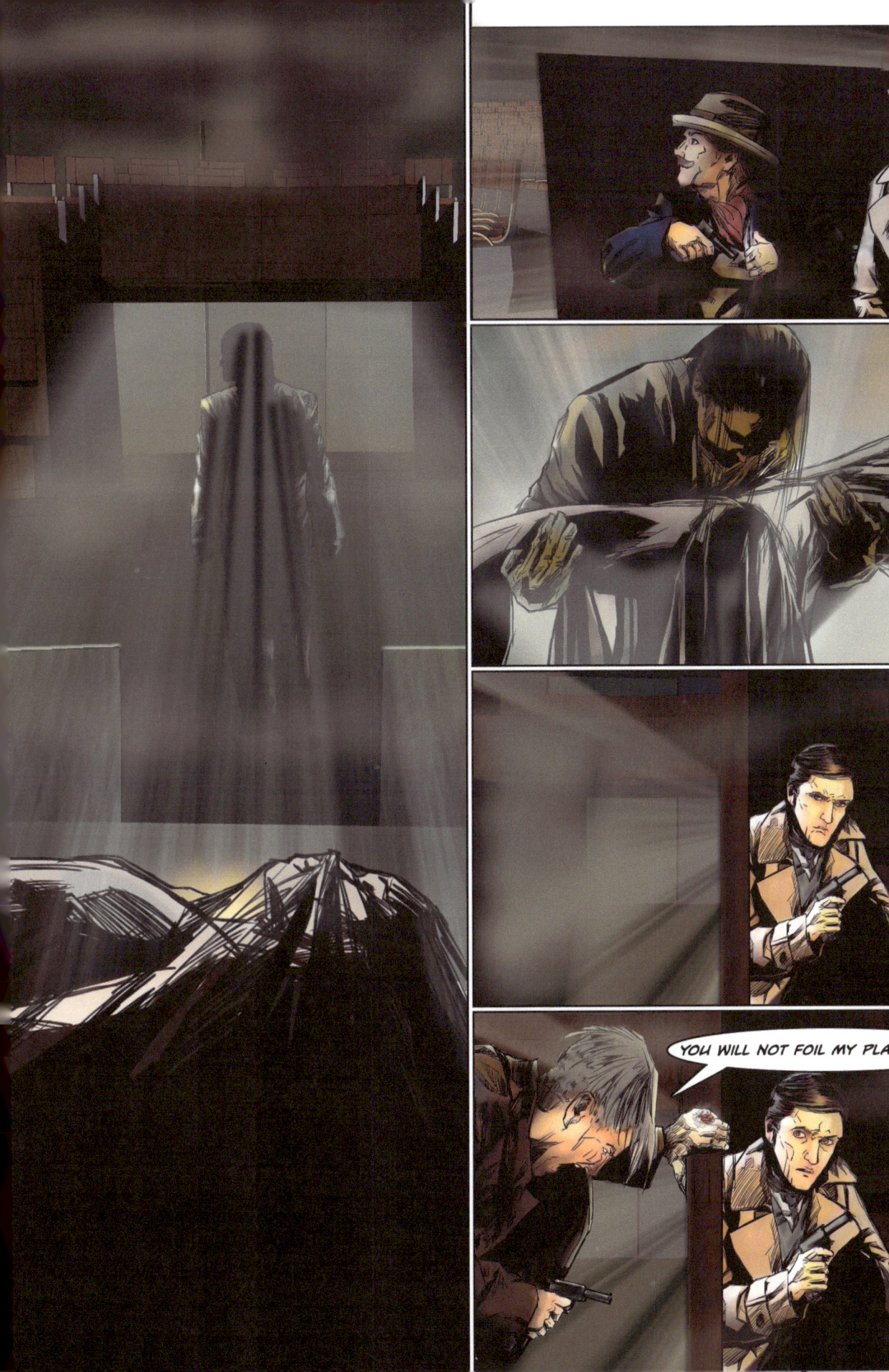

CRAAACK

WELL, THIS IS JUST DANDY.

I HAVE AN INJURED MAN, HOLMES, I MUST SEE TO THAT AND THIS BROKEN MARIA.

TIME IS PRECIOUS, INSPECTOR. WE MUST CARRY ON!

I'M SORRY, BUT WE MUST KEEP GOING! YOU DO WHAT YOU MUST, WE'LL BE AT PRETORIUS'S CASTLE.

OFFICER WILLIAMS, YOU TAKE THE HORSE AND FETCH US SOME AID. I'LL STAY WITH JONES TILL YOU RETURN. WHEN YOU GET BACK WE'LL MEET UP WITH HOLMES AT THE CASTLE.

YOU SHOULD HAVE LEFT ME BURIED IN THE ICE.

I WANTED TO GIVE YOU LIFE, GIVE YOU EVERYTHING THAT FRANKENSTEIN FAILED TO GIVE.

YOU ... WANT POWER

YOU WANT ... TO BE A GOD.

GET US OUT OF HERE! YOU CAN GO FREE! YOU CAN FORGET ME AND I'LL FORGET YOU!

WE ARE CREATURES BORN OUT OF DEATH AND DEATH IS ALL THAT COMES FROM US!

BAM

# ALSO FROM LUKE BENJAMEN KUHNS & MARCIE KLINGER

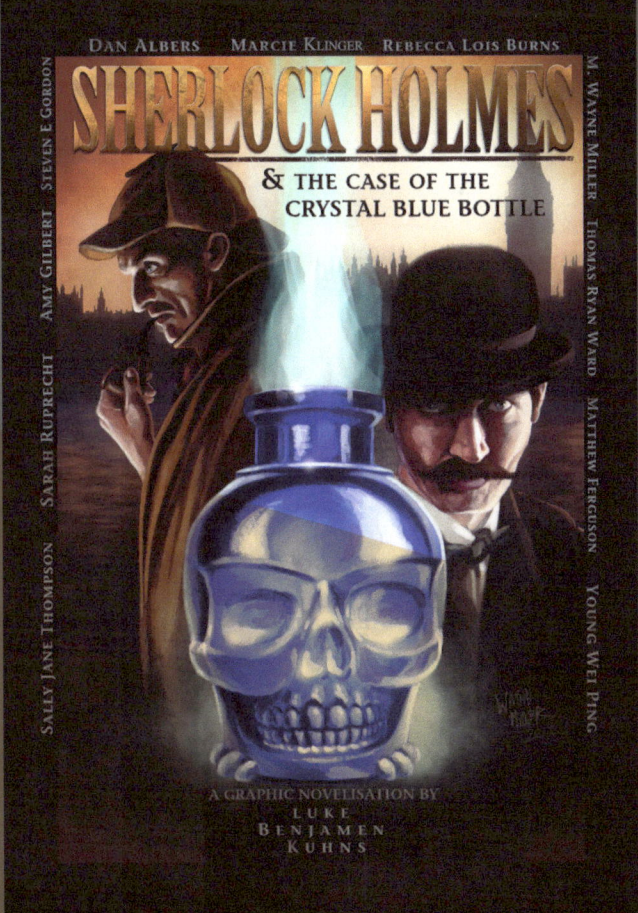

SHERLOCK HOLMES
& THE CASE OF THE CRYSTAL BLUE BOTTLE
A GRAPHIC NOVEL

AVAILABLE IN PAPERBACK AND EBOOK FROM ALL GOOD BOOK STORES IN US & UK AND ON AMAZON.COM, AMAZON.CO.UK AND THE BOOK DEPOSITORY ! ALTERNATIVELY YOU CAN ORDER STRAIGHT FROM MX PUBLISHING!

A YOUNG WOMAN NAMED DESERAY UNDERWOOD HAS BEEN FOUND DEAD, IN HER LONDON LODGINGS, BY HER FIANCE SAMUEL MORTIMER. THE BODY ITSELF SHOWS NO SIGNS OF A STRUGGLE. LESTRADE, BAFFLED BY THE CAUSE OF DEATH, SUMMONS THE AID OF SHERLOCK HOLMES AND HIS GREAT POWERS OF DEDUCTION. HOLMES STUMBLES UPON ONE SINGLE CLUE, A CRYSTAL BLUE BOTTLE, WHICH SENDS HIM AND WATSON ON A WILD CHASE THROUGH THE STREETS OF LONDON IN PURSUIT OF ANSWERS TO THIS YOUNG WOMAN'S SUDDEN DEMISE. A DEATH THAT WOULD MAKE ANY BENEFACTOR VERY WEALTHY.

FEATURING 11 OUTSTANDING ILLUSTRATORS FROM ACROSS THE GLOBE, THE STORY COMES TO LIFE THROUGH THE EFFORTS OF REBECCA BURNS, MARCIE KLINGER, AND SARAH RUPRECHT & DAN ALBERS. ALONG WITH CONTRIBUTIONS FROM HIGH PROFILE ILLUSTRATORS STEVEN E. GORDON (THE GREAT MOUSE DETECTIVE, X-MEN EVOLUTION, ULTIMATE AVENGERS), MATTHEW FERGUSON (MARVEL'S THE AVENGERS, STAR WARS & CHRONICLE) & WAYNE MILLER (SHERLOCK HOLMES REVENANT ILLUSTRATOR).

# ALSO FROM LUKE BENJAMEN KUHNS

SHERLOCK HOLMES: STUDIES IN LEGACY IS AVAILABLE IN PAPERBACK AND EBOOK FROM ALL GOOD BOOK STORES INCLUDING USA BARNES AND NOBLE, AMAZON, & ITUNES. IN THE UK WATERSTONES, AMAZON UK, & ITUNES UK. FOR FANS OUTSIDE THE US/UK YOU CAN GET FREE DELIVERY FROM THE BOOK DEPOSITORY.

"THERE IS NOTHING MORE TRAGIC THAN A STORY LEFT UNTOLD. AT LEAST THAT IS WHAT SHERLOCK HOLMES THOUGHT. THROUGH HIS URGINGS DOCTOR WATSON OPENS HIS TIN DISPATCH BOX TO RECALL A SERIES OF STRANGE AND GROTESQUE EVENTS WHICH CONSUMED THEIR DAILY LIVES IN THE EARLY MONTHS OF 1899. FOLLOW HOLMES AND WATSON AS THEY TACKLE AN UNUSUAL CASE OF HYSTERIA, RACE THROUGH FIRES IN WHITECHAPEL, FIND MYSTERY AND MURDER IN A SEASIDE VILLAGE, AND DISCOVER WHAT STRANGE GAME IS AFOOT WHEN AN ASSAULT IN THE CONFINES OF 221B SENDS HOLMES AND WATSON RACING AGAINST TIME TOWARDS A DEADLY AND TOXIC END! ONE THING IS CERTAIN, SOMETIMES THE MOST DEADLY VILLAIN IS THEIR LEGACY."
THE UNTOLD ADVENTURES OF SHERLOCK HOLMES – VOL. 2

THE UNTOLD ADVENTURES OF SHERLOCK HOLMES IS AVAILABLE IN PAPERBACK AND EBOOK FROM ALL GOOD BOOKSTORES INCLUDING IN THE USA BARNES AND NOBLE, AMAZON & ITUNES. IN THE UK AMAZON, WATERSTONES, ITUNES UK. FOR FANS OUTSIDE US AND UK CAN GET FREE DELIVERY FROM BOOK DEPOSITORY. ALTERNATIVELY YOU CAN ORDER STRAIGHT FROM MX PUBLISHING!

IN THE UNTOLD ADVENTURES OF SHERLOCK HOLMES DOCTOR WATSON RECALLS SEVEN ADVENTURES THAT HE ACCOMPANIED HIS FRIEND MR SHERLOCK HOLMES ON. IN THIS BOOK HOLMES AND WATSON ARE CAUGHT IN THE MIDDLE OF GOVERNMENT SCANDALS, COLD BLOODED MURDERS, THREATS FROM BEYOND OUR REALM, AND IN A STORY THAT WORKS THROUGH OVER A DECADE OF HOLMES'S CASES WE LEARN A LITTLE BIT MORE ABOUT THE MYSTERY THAT SURROUNDS WATSON'S WIFE, MARY AND WHAT BECAME OF HER SUDDEN DISAPPEARANCE FROM WATSON'S LIFE..

www.ingramcontent.com/pod-product-compliance
Lightning Source LLC
Chambersburg PA
CBHW041004170626
46815CB00002B/157